Discord
✶✶✶ and ✶✶✶
The Ponyville Players Dramarama

Written by G. M. Berrow

Little, Brown and Company
New York Boston

Little, Brown and Company

Hachette Book Group
1290 Avenue of the Americas, New York, NY 10104
Visit us at lb-kids.com

Little, Brown and Company is a division of Hachette Book Group, Inc. The Little, Brown name and logo are trademarks of Hachette Book Group, Inc.

The publisher is not responsible for websites (or their content) that are not owned by the publisher.

First Edition: July 2015

ISBN 978-0-316-41083-0

10 9 8 7 6 5 4 3 2 1

RRD-C

Printed in the United States of America

For Banzai, who was
the best kind of chaos

CONTENTS

* * *

Chapter

1

The Open Market

* * *

It was a peculiar day in Ponyville. No, it wasn't one of those days where everything was just perfect and dandy. There was a slight crookedness to the position of the sun, an intangible strangeness to the shape of the clouds, and a funny *feeling* going around. Though, it is true that the day had begun like any other. First, with Princess Celestia raising the sun from her royal balcony in Canterlot. Everywhere across Equestria, ponies woke and began their days. In Ponyville, it always started with the sound of birds chirping their sweet morning song, followed by the bustle and shuffle of the little schoolponies trying not to be late for their first lesson, and finally, the townsponies trotting to their various social and work engagements with expectant smiles upon their faces.

Then, sometime around midmorning, it all went wrong. The familiar, wicked laughter started out soft, but grew louder with each minute. It echoed through the alleyways and whispered through the windowpanes of every cottage, café, and cake shop in town. The sound sent shivers down the townsponies' spines, and sent them galloping straight back to their homes, waiting for the storm of chaos to pass.

But there was really nothing to fear. Discord the draconequus, the king of chaos and former tormentor of ponies, was now *reformed*—of all things! Unfortunately, he only had enough pony friends to count on one claw and one paw, so the residents of Ponyville still believed him to be an unpredictable terror. In fact, he was still unpredictable, but a little less of a terror.

"How unexpected of me to show up today!" he said, strolling through the streets with glee. "It's been far too long." Discord hadn't visited Ponyville for a long while. The last time he'd popped up in town to see his new friends—Fluttershy, Princess

Twilight Sparkle, Pinkie Pie, Applejack, Rainbow Dash, and Rarity—he'd scared the colts and fillies of the school just by floating past. Discord's friends had tried to comfort the young ponies and their angry parents, insisting that Discord meant them no harm. But the townsponies were still uneasy. What sort of kooky magic could he unleash on them for his own amusement? Would it be turning their homes upside down and lifting them into the sky? Perhaps Discord would transform the pet bunnies into scary long-legged creatures again! Or maybe he would simply change the order of the streets to watch the ponies stand there, scratching their manes in confusion, lost in their own town.

But Discord was not in Ponyville to cause trouble. He was here on a special, secret assignment. He took out the crumpled scroll that bore the Canterlot Castle crest and read it once again.

Dear Discord,

I'm glad to hear reports that you've been living well in Chaosville. Please send my kind regards to The Smooze. As you and I both know, your road to learning about the Magic of Friendship has been a rocky one. But one's path in life is often full of detours, such as the incident involving Tirek. Today,

I write to grant you an opportunity
that I feel would further enrich
your experience as a friend to all of
ponykind.

This spring, the residents of
Ponyville will join together for a
common goal—the Spring Musical.
I want you to partake in this
community effort. If you are able to
prove that you have worked as part of
a team to make this event a success,
I will gladly return a token of yours

from days past. For it is only then that I can trust your commitment to becoming a permanent ally of Equestria.

Your Friend,

Princess Celestia

P.S. Do not tell anypony of this task.

When he'd received the letter at his cottage in Chaosville, Discord wasn't sure what to do. He lived a quiet life in his tidy house. Why should he turn everything upside down just to help some little ponies?

But then Discord remembered that he loved flipping things upside down, and also that he was quite bored. And then there was the little matter of this "item." What could it be?

Discord had hidden several personal treasures and relics around Canterlot during his brief, chaotic reign over Equestria. In the days since he'd been freed from his statue in the gardens, he'd located almost all of them. Apparently, he was *too* good at hiding things, because a few still eluded the draconequus. If Celestia had accidentally found a simple-looking stone orb marked with the Crest of Chaos some-where in the depths of the castle dungeons, then he would do anything to get it back. Discord's heart quickened when he imagined holding it in his paw and claw once more.

But as much as he wanted his long-lost relic, Discord started to regret his decision to rush straight into town. He uselessly floated and aimlessly strolled and soon found himself just outside the Ponyville marketplace. Two Earth ponies trotted by with wagons hitched to their backs. They each had flowers for cutie marks and fresh bouquets of roses and lilies piled high in their wagons.

"A good day to you both," said Discord, bowing dramatically and tipping a green top hat that had just appeared on his head out of nowhere. But rather than return his greeting, the flower salesponies screamed in horror and galloped back in the direction they'd come, leaving a trail of petals in their wake. "How rude!" Discord said, furrowing his bushy eyebrows. He picked up a fallen red rose and sniffed it. "With all the times I've visited, I practically live here in Ponyville! And yet these little ponies act as if they've never met me before."

"Would ya like to live here?!" a scratchy voice exclaimed. "I can help with that."

"Help with what?" Discord spun around. A stout yellow Unicorn with a thinning orange mane parted on one side had appeared. He had a cutie mark of a thatched cottage and a sneaky smile on his face. The pony held out his hoof, but Discord didn't touch it.

"The name's Martingale," the pony said. "And sellin' houses is my business. I can get ya into a new place as soon as today."

Martingale grinned, adding a wink for good measure. "If you're interested, of course."

"It seems that you've popped up at the perfect time," Discord answered. "Something's about to happen in Ponyville, and I must stick around for it."

Chapter

2

great
Potential!

★ ★ ★

"So," Discord said as he followed Martingale. "What marvelous houses do you have to show the all-powerful king of chaos today?"

This was the first showing Martingale had booked in weeks, and he was silently cursing his luck that it had turned out to be for Discord, of all characters. He wasn't quite sure if he trusted the beast after everything he'd done throughout history, but still, he needed a sale. Desperately.

"Ah yes, there it is on the corner!" Martingale pointed his hoof and straightened his purple polka-dot tie. "Right this way, Mr. Discord."

Discord gasped as the house came into view. "Why, it's hideous!" He put his left eagle claw over his mouth in shock. Below it, a devilish smirk began to form.

"Well, it *is* a bit of a fixer-upper, but the place has great potential," explained Martingale with a forced smile. "Lots of light. And the garden is top-notch, I assure you! Just *top-notch*. You're gonna love it! Just let me check something first." The yellow Unicorn stallion trotted to the side of the house and peeked at the back garden. It was overgrown with weeds, and several anthills had sprung up since his last visit to the wretched property. "I mean, the front garden is the one with the nice, er...view," he improvised. "Go ahead, sir. Take a look yourself."

"I do love a good view," Discord admitted, and floated his brown, snake-like body up to the side of the second floor. He crossed his legs, lounging back on an invisible chair to take in the surroundings. He wrinkled his nose. All he could see was the back of another quaint cottage.

"That house is blocking my view," Discord noted. "I'll just have to move it."

"Well, I don't know if the neighbors would like *that* very much but—"

"The neighbors!" Discord laughed. "How pleasant. They'll learn to cooperate quite quickly, don't you think?" Discord snapped his claw, and the house magically shifted over to the next street. A scream came from inside the cottage. Martingale chuckled nervously and loosened his tie.

"Unless you have another house to show me?" Discord asked with a smile.

"Actually, no," Martingale admitted. "Ponyville is very popular at the moment. There was a bit of a housing boom after Princess Twilight's castle showed up. Not that we had too many empty cottages to begin with...." Martingale slumped down.

"Is that so?" The draconequus raised one of his bushy white eyebrows and stared down the Unicorn. "And all that's left is this hideous monstrosity on the edge of town? Surely you can do better than this, Mr. Nightingale."

"It's Martingale—"

"Look, this house is in absolute shambles," exclaimed Discord with a smirk, throwing his arms up. The beast pretended to scowl. He began to float back and forth in the air, pointing his one lion's paw at each of the property's many flaws. "The shutters are falling off, the floorboards are wonky, and the color is absolutely *atrocious*."

"So is that a no?" Martingale tried to hide his disappointment, but his face had begun to form a frown.

"On the contrary..." Discord cackled.

"It's perfect!" He spun around and magically appeared in a fancy pin-striped business suit and shoes with spats. "Care to make a deal?"

Chapter

3

Home Chaotic Home

★ ★ ★

"Thank Celestia, I never thought I'd get this dud off my hooves...." Martingale let out a sigh of relief and smiled. "I mean— this is a top-notch property, it is! *Ahem.*"

"Bits or IOU?" Discord asked, and dumped out his wallet onto the dying grass in the front yard. Three pebbles, several candy wrappers, an old smelly boot, and a pack of spinach-flavored dental floss fell out. "Well, barn it. No bits on me. IOU, it is," chuckled Discord, leading the confused pony up the front walk and outside the picket fence. "Not to worry, old chap, I've got stacks and stacks upon towers of them back in Chaosville. As soon as I pop back there to grab my essentials, you'll have it in your hot little hooves."

Martingale frowned. "But I only take bits...."

"Be right backsies!" The draconequus disappeared with a loud *Pop!* Martingale had barely registered what had happened before the beast reappeared once more. Only this time, a mountain of boxes labeled with the words NEW PONYVILLE HOUSE accompanied him. He sauntered past them and passed a slip of beet-juice-stained parchment to the pony.

"What's this?" Martingale began squinting as he read it aloud robotically. "*I, Discord, the most powerful and chaotic resident of Ponyville, owe you one unique payment of my choosing, payable upon my full satisfaction of the premises and experience here, also*—hey! Wait right there…"

"Ah, ah, ah!" Discord singsonged as he wagged his pointy claw, magically zipping the lips of the stallion. "No arguing, Random Inconsequential Pony." Martingale tried to speak but the words couldn't escape. He just sounded muffled and annoyed.

"What's that?" teased Discord. He held

his lion's paw to his right ear and leaned down so that his deer antler almost brushed the pony's orange mane. "It's a deal? Great!" Discord pointed at the pony's foreleg, and he magically obeyed, lifting his hoof and pressing it to a tie-dyed rainbow inkpad. Martingale struggled against the spell, but he couldn't resist placing it on the contract. Discord smiled and swished his claw to the left, through the air. Suddenly his signature, resembling a tornado, appeared on the scroll as well. "Splendid!" A red SOLD sign swung down from the one that said FOR SALE.

"But I didn't want to make that deal!" Martingale's words spilled out of his mouth as soon as they were unzipped. He trotted up to Discord and shoved the parchment at him with a frown. "And you didn't even pay me!"

"Then why did you agree to do business with me, silly fellow?"

Martingale's eyes darted around in a panic as he searched for an answer that might not make the situation worse. But when he opened his mouth to speak, nothing came out.

"Cat got your tongue again?" Discord giggled. He floated over a black-and-white kitty that was batting something small and pink around. Martingale galloped over, distraught. "Muhhh uuung!"

Discord rolled his eyes and clapped his claw and paw together. The tongue was magically returned to Martingale's mouth.

"Stop stealing my ability to speak, you...

you…beast!" Martingale stomped his yellow hoof into the dirt. "I should have never shown you any houses in Ponyville at all, not even this one. You just bring chaos everywhere you go!"

"Chaos? *Moi?*" Discord batted his extra large yellow eyes with mismatched red pupils. A glowing halo materialized above his horns. "When have I ever been involved in a thing like that?" The perpetual smirk on his lips couldn't hold itself back.

The pony scoffed. "There's no way that this contract is legally binding. I'm taking this to the mayor!"

Discord began to unpack his first box, labeled with a sticker that said LEFT SOCKS AND KITCHEN SINKS. "Oh, goody, it'll save me the trouble of going over there. Tell her I can't wait until our bridge game on Thursday afternoon. I'm bringing the seven-layer bean dip."

Martingale grumbled something to himself as he trotted away toward town hall.

"Toodles! Do consider bringing back a noodle casserole to welcome me to the neighborhood!" Discord shouted with a gleeful smile. Then he turned on his hoof and surveyed his front lawn, beginning to visualize the improvements that needed to be made to the grounds.

Soon, things were looking much more haphazard and ugly, which was such a relief. Discord was proud of the purple and yellow zigzags he'd painted on the exterior, the collection of broken kitchen sinks now arranged in the front garden, and the variety of squeaks and creaks he'd added to the floor so that each step was a symphony of utter unpleasantness to the ears.

Discord smiled to himself as he unpacked the last box, containing a tea set that had been a Hearth's Warming gift from Fluttershy. It was the only pretty thing he owned. In all honesty, he actually found it quite unsightly, but he cherished it because it represented his very first friend.

"That reminds me," Discord mused. "The only thing this house needs now is somepony to laugh and gossip with. Then it will be nauseatingly perfect." He snapped his claws and teleported to a familiar little cottage on the outskirts of Ponyville.

"Oh, Fluttershyyyy!" he called out, skipping toward the door and causing all the tiny birds to fly away in surprise. "You'll never guess who just moved to Ponyville." He knocked on the door three times, but there was no answer. So he kicked down the door. "It's me! Now your best pal Discord is only a hop, skip, and a jump away from you at all times." But nopony replied. In fact, it was completely dark inside. A basket of sleeping kittens stretched themselves awake, and a pair of ferrets came out of a small toy tunnel and yawned. "Ah, of course. It's afternoon naptime for the critters. Fluttershy always goes out then so she doesn't disturb them." Discord scratched his white goatee in deep thought. "Where could that little winged lemon drop be today?"

A door swung open, and Angel Bunny appeared, looking nothing short of annoyed. He frowned and thrust out his tiny white paw at the massive intruder, shoving a colorful piece of paper into Discord's left goat's hoof.

"What's this, my fretful, furry, fairweather friend?" Discord's eyes quickly scanned the page. "Fluttershy's at the auditions for the Ponyville Players Spring Musical?" Discord's eyes grew wide. "That's my cue!"

Angel Bunny crossed his arms over his chest and hopped onto a big red button that slammed the door right in Discord's face. "Well, that was quite rude. Bad bunny!" Discord sent a zap of magic through the window that caused Angel's legs to grow as tall as a giraffe's. Discord chuckled as he watched the bunny wobble around in confusion, and then changed him back to normal again. It was an old trick, but a classic one.

"It feels so strange to be living in Ponyville," Discord marveled as he floated off toward the theater. "But I think I can make it work." He spent the rest of the trip thinking of all the delicious ways that one might cause mischief during a stage production. There were far too many to count, which was just the right number for him.

Chapter

4

The Ponyville Players

★ ★ ★

Discord watched from afar as the eager thespian ponies filed into the entrance of the theater, dressed in their finest audition clothes. Discord rolled his eyes. "How dreadful. But...I *suppose* I must look the part as well if I'm to impress these picky little ponies. Especially that Rarity." With a tap of his toe, Discord was draped from head to tail in his most dramatic outfit—a billowy white shirt, a brown velvet waistcoat, and black pants that puffed out like two balloons. Around his neck was a frilly white ruff that extended far past his shoulders. "Now they'll take me seriously."

As Discord made his way into the theater, he took no notice of the scared onlookers darting away at the sight of him. Many townsponies had chalked up the news of Discord moving into Ponyville to be a silly rumor. But he was actually here! "Ahhhh!" screamed Sea Swirl, a light purple Unicorn with a cutie mark of two dolphins. She dropped some script pages on the ground and took off in a gallop toward Sugarcube Corner.

"Thanks for the sides!" Discord shouted

as he snagged the papers and waltzed inside to join the line backstage.

He managed to remain unnoticed by the panel of pony judges seated in the audience as he pushed his way through the dusty-smelling red curtains. "Teehee!" he laughed to himself, thinking of the big reveal. Now that he had two surprises—his big move to Ponyville and his soon-to-be starring role in their little production—he was bubbling over with enthusiasm. The look on Twilight Sparkle's face when she saw him onstage was going to be priceless! She might even pass out from shock.

Discord wanted to get the show on the road, but unfortunately, there were about five ponies ahead of him waiting to go onstage. One of them was Cheerilee, the teacher from Ponyville School. The mauve

Earth pony had her light pink mane crimped in a style that Discord hadn't seen in a long while. Around her neck was a black-and-white-checkered scarf, and she wore a scrunched neon leg warmer on each back hoof.

"Reliving your lost youth, are you dear?" Discord teased, popping up next to Cheerilee out of nowhere. He grinned and pointed to his own ancient costume. "Me too!" Discord giggled. "Get it? Because I'm thousands of years old?"

Cheerilee shook her head with a patronizing frown, trotting off to wait in the wings and stretch. "Well, I thought it was funny," Discord said, shrugging. A moment later, Cheerilee pranced out onto the stage. She introduced herself and began to belt out a rendition of the classic pop hit,

"Fillies Just Wanna Have Fun." Discord bopped up and down to the music for a few seconds before it hit him: He didn't have a song prepared! How were the judges going to take him seriously if he didn't even have music to showcase his incredible talents? And if he wasn't cast in the show, how would he complete Celestia's mission? And if he didn't accomplish the mission, how would he get his beloved thing back?

"What are *you* doing here, Discord?!" A pink pony with a curly fuchsia mane popped up next to him, interrupting his internal panic and causing him to jump a little.

"Pinkie Pie! You startled me!" Discord replied. He crossed his arms over his velvet vest. *"Very impressive."*

"Thanks! Sometimes I get started

startling ponies before I've even finished finishing." Pinkie Pie giggled. "Oooh, is that a ruffle-puff collar you're wearing? It's the silliest piece of clothing I've ever seen!" Pinkie's eyes grew wide as she tilted her head. "Can I borrow it?"

"I don't see why not. Or..." Discord snapped his claws, and suddenly Pinkie Pie was wearing a ruffled-collar so big that it covered most of her body. It looked like a giant pink and blue tutu.

"Yippeee!!" She smiled and began to bounce up and down so that the fabric flapped.

Discord sighed. "Happy now?"

"I'm happy *always*." The pink pony nod-ded. "But since you asked...you know what would make me *even happier*? Like super ecstatic-electricity, frosting-for-breakfast, swimming-in-summertime happy? Some of that yummilicious chocolate rain you make." Pinkie licked her lips and danced around to Cheerilee's song. When it ended a few seconds later, Discord turned back to Pinkie.

"What were you saying?" Discord asked, scratching his goatee pensively. "I stopped listening. After a while, high-pitched pony chatter just sounds like buzzing to me."

"Or maybe you spaced out because you're worried since you didn't practice a song for the audition." Pinkie Pie shrugged. "It is a super big problem, so I understand."

"You caught me. I know so many amazing songs," Discord jutted out his bottom lip so that his snaggletooth poked out even farther. "But how to choose one with so little time?"

"You could always sing that great song about the glass of water," Pinkie suggested. She stroked her hoof against her chin in deep thought. "But you'd have to catch the Blue Flu again first...."

"That *was* a brilliant performance of mine. Even so—it's been done. It's been *seen*." Discord shook his head. "I need something fresh!" He looked out to the stage. Little pieces of neon yellow, green, and pink paper confetti littered the expanse of the entire floor from the final note of Cheerilee's number, and a bored stagehoof was sweeping it up. "I need something where I can set the scene like Cheerilee did. Something with pizzazz!"

"Maybe something involving chocolate rain?" Pinkie Pie asked, leaning in closer to Discord to whisper. *"Chocolate. Rain."*

"That's it, Pinkie Pie!" Discord chuckled. He looked up to the ceiling rafters with a new determination. "I'll perform the one classic award-winning musical favorite that's sure to impress and delight everypony in all of Ponyville…'Singin' in the Chocolate Rain'!"

"That's perfect!" shouted Pinkie Pie with a loud squeal. "I mean…good idea. Need any help?"

Chapter

5

Don't Judge an Audition Before It's Over

★ ★ ★

"Wow! That was great!" Twilight whispered, turning to her fellow judges with a cheesy grin. "What did you all think about Cheerilee's performance?" The Ponyville Players Audition Committee sat beside her watching the aspiring actors perform one by one for a part in *The Singing Stallion* from their seats in the audience. Toe Tapper and Rarity, two members of the Ponytones quartet, smiled in agreement. Senior Mint, a tall green Pegasus and lead member of the Ponyville Choir, hummed the tune of "Fillies Just Want to Have Fun" and gave Twilight a wink.

"Fantastic. I'll add her to the list of favorites for a lead role, then," announced Twilight, satisfied.

"Are we ready to move on to the next hopeful?" Fluttershy asked. Torch Song nodded as she finished writing in her score sheet. "Next pony, please!" Fluttershy tried to shout toward the stage, but it came out very softly. A moment passed, and nopony appeared.

"Next pony, please!" Twilight Sparkle

announced, a bit louder. But instead of another pony trotting out, both the stage and house lights went completely black. Then, all they could hear was the sound of raucous laughter. It grew louder and louder with each moment until finally, a searing spotlight beamed down to reveal the source. It was none other than Discord himself!

"I'm he-ee-ere!" he announced with vibrato. "Though, the pony part is debatable."

The draconequus was now dressed in a blue suit, and wore a jaunty hat with his horns poking through the top. His purple dragon wing and blue Pegasus wing sprouted out of the back of his jacket, and in his left claw he held a large umbrella. Discord leaned on it as if it were a cane and smiled at the judges. Then, he floated into the air, popped the umbrella open, and leaned his face on his lion paw underneath it.

"Discord! What are you doing here?" Twilight exclaimed, standing up on her hooves. "Can't you see we're in the middle of our Ponyville Players auditions right now?"

"Why, of course I can, dear Princess," Discord replied. "And that is precisely why I'm here—to audition for a role in the Spring Musical!" Discord floated back down to the ground with a playful smirk on his face. The purple pony was even more steamed than he'd anticipated. It was deliciously amusing.

"Come on, Discord," Twilight begged. "Stop messing around, okay?" She held up a scroll with a long list of names scribbled on it. "We have a lot of ponies to get through today, and we want to make sure they all get their chance to try out." She motioned her hoof to the theater door and raised a brow. "This show is a really big deal for us here in Ponyville. The other princesses are going to be in attendance and—"

"Really, Twilight…" Discord floated over to the judges' table, nonchalant. "I thought you'd all be pleased as punch to have me here." A bowl of fruit punch magically appeared on the table. Discord ladled some into a cup and slurped it up in one gulp. He ladled a few more and passed them to Senior Mint and Toe Tapper, who both took hesitant sips. "With my musical talents and incredible stage presence, you'd practically have to be fools not to cast me in your production."

Discord handed Twilight a cup of punch, but she pushed it away in annoyance. "Actually, the last time you stood on a stage to perform, it was a trick," said Twilight. "You were working for Tirek and stealing all the Unicorn magic in the auditorium to use it for your evil plot." She raised a suspicious eyebrow. "How do we know you haven't got some ulterior motive this time, too?" She turned to the others for support, but they were all sipping punch and looked mildly intrigued by the audition-crasher.

"Those days are far behind me, I assure you." Discord sat on the judges' table like a lounge singer on a piano. "Plus, there's no point in arguing about the issue. You simply *have* to let me audition."

"And why is that?" Rarity asked, attempting to show her support for Twilight Sparkle. While it was true that Discord had redeemed himself a number of times, the ponies knew that they should still be a little bit cautious around him. Even if his suit *was* all sorts of fabulous. Rarity tried to ignore the intricate stitching and matching pocket square.

"Because, Rarity, darling, it's in the *rules*." Discord thrust the flyer into her face. "Right there, in teensy-weensy print at the bottom it says, 'All residents of Ponyville who wish to audition are welcome.'"

"So it does," Rarity said, inspecting the fine print with her red cat-eye reading glasses. "But you don't live in Ponyville."

"That's why you sleep on my sofa when you need a nap after our Tuesday Teas,"

Fluttershy said in her tiny voice. "I don't mind, though," she added just to make sure she didn't hurt his feelings. "True friends always let each other nap."

"And as much as I'll miss that tradition, Fluttershy, I'm happy to announce that I moved into Ponyville today!" Discord giggled with glee as the jaws of the ponies dropped in shock. "It's true. Just ask Pinkie Pie."

"It's true! He did!" Pinkie Pie bounced out onto the stage, still wearing her fluffy tutu. "Now, let him audition! I need that sweet, sweet rain."

Twilight Sparkle looked to her fellow judges. Nopony seemed to have a valid reason to refuse Discord an audition. Twilight rolled her eyes and plopped back down in her chair. "I guess I'm outnumbered. This performance had better be entertaining."

"Prepare to be razzled and dazzled *and* frazzled...." Discord snapped his claw as he floated back to his place center stage. The hooflights came up as a storm of pink clouds formed above him. The music started low and grew louder. *"Doodle doo doo doo, doodle doo doo doo doo,"* sang Discord, sashaying back and forth across the stage with his umbrella in his claw and paw. Giant drops of liquid chocolate started to rain down on him. *"I'm singin' in the chocolate rain! Just siiiiiingin' in the chocolate rain! An uproarious ceiling, I'm tappin' agaa-aa-ain!"* Discord did a shuffle-ball-change, and the sound of metal clacked on the wooden stage. *"I'm cackling at clouds, so pink up abo-oo-ove."* A lamppost appeared onstage, and Discord jumped onto it. He leaned out, holding on with his lion's paw. *"The song's in my heart, and I'm ready for gruuuub!"* A sandwich appeared, and he took a bite as he danced.

Pinkie Pie couldn't help herself and joined him on the stage, dancing to the song and taking large gulps of chocolate rain with each bounce. After three more verses, Discord took off his hat and slid forward on his knees for the big finish. He belted out the last lyrics. *"Just singin' and prancin' in the chocolate raa-aa-aain!"*

He looked out to the judges with a charming smirk, and the ponies couldn't help but smile back. Even Twilight Sparkle cracked a grin. As they all cheered, he beamed with pride. "So, when does the casting notice go up?"

"An audition does not guarantee a spot," warned Twilight.

"Oh, of course not." Discord smiled and winked. He tried to act humble, even though he knew he had just scored the lead role. "Not everypony has what it takes, unfortunately."

Torch Song cleared her throat. "We'll be visiting ponies around town tomorrow to let them know of our casting decisions."

Discord clapped. "Oh, goody."

"But, Discord?" Twilight furrowed her brow and looked him straight in the eye.

"Yes, Princess?"

"Don't call on us; we'll call on *you*, okay?"

Chapter

6

Role Call

★ ★ ★

The next day seemed to creep by slower than the hundreds of years Discord had spent trapped in a stone statue in the Canterlot gardens. Waiting to hear of the Ponyville Players casting decisions was torturously boring. All day long, Discord floated back and forth across his kitchen.

He tumbled up and down the stairs, did headstands on the ceiling, and even took a bubble bath.

At one point, Martingale the real estate pony came by, looking nervous. He prattled on, mumbling something about the house not being for sale anymore. "Fella, I think we've had a misunderstandin'," he tried to say. But instead of talking to the chap, Discord turned himself into a gigantic, scary spider and dropped down in the doorframe. Martingale screamed and went running off into town.

Aside from that encounter, nothing amused Discord much, so he turned to more extreme measures. He uprooted the whole house, turning it upside down. The building drifted around in a circle, suspended in the air by magic. Discord watched from the windows as ponies would trot by, see the house, and then scatter immediately. It was good for one or two chuckles. By the late afternoon, however, Discord had become so stir-crazy that he decided he could take it no longer. Ponyville was just on the other side of his walls. Surely something interesting could happen out there.

"Whom shall I tinker with today?" Discord said as he flung open the door and looked out to Ponyville below. "Mr. and Mrs. Cake? Nurse Redheart?"

"Nopony!" a voice shouted, much to his surprise. Standing down on the ground, staring up at his abode, were none other than all seven of his best Ponyville friends:

Twilight Sparkle, Fluttershy, Pinkie Pie, Rainbow Dash, Applejack, Rarity, and Spike. "Discord," Twilight shouted up at the floating house. "Come down from there! We have to talk."

"Hey, I like what you've done with the place," said Pinkie Pie. "Very jazzy."

"I'm afraid I must disagree with you," Rarity said, wrinkling her nose. "That paint color is very ill-advised."

"Rarity, how kind! That's just the look I was going for." Discord smiled sincerely, motioning to the house. "But you haven't even seen the best part yet—the interior design! I did it with guests in mind. Won't you all come inside for a cup of tea?"

Before the ponies and dragon could answer his invitation, Discord pointed his claw at them. They all rose up toward the front door, encased in a glowing, purple bubble of magic. Applejack rolled her eyes at the stunt. "Ya coulda just lowered the buildin' back to the ground, *where it belongs.* Why's everything gotta be such a big show with you?"

"Because I was born for show business, Appleshack." Discord clasped his claw and paw together, setting the ponies down in front of the rickety kitchen table and mismatched chairs. "Which is why, I presume, you're all here to visit me? Go ahead, you can tell me that I got the lead role in the Ponyville Players musical. No need to sing and dance around the subject."

A dented copper kettle whistled on the stove.

The ponies all exchanged an awkward look. "Oh, uhh...what makes you think you got the lead?" Rainbow Dash shifted in her chair. Her eyes darted around. "I mean— how do you know?"

"When you know, you just *know*," said Discord, raising his bushy eyebrows.

He began to whistle a happy tune as he poured eight cups of steaming liquid all at once. Fluttershy smiled and took a sip of hers. "Mmmm, I love chamomile," she cooed. Nopony else moved. Discord sat down.

"So will I be portraying Captain Von Scrapp in *Hinny of the Hills*? Pone Valpone in *Les Miser Stables*? Oooh! What about Corny Cauliflower in *Manespray*? I do love that character. Such flair."

"No, we're actually doing a production of the old small-town favorite, *The Singing Stallion*," Twilight replied, her voice perky.

"And you're in the show! Isn't that great news, Discord?"

"It's not news, since I already knew I was the best," replied Discord. "And though the role of Professor Hayloft Shill is not my favorite lead to play, I'll make it work."

"You're not playing the role of Hayloft," said Rarity, making a sympathetic face. "Sorry, dear."

Discord's face fell. "Then who is?"

Chapter

7

No Small Parts

✦ ✦ ✦

Discord had to rub his ears to make sure he wasn't hearing things. "BIG MAC?!" he exclaimed, jaw to the floor. "But he only knows two words!"

"Big Mac was just right for the part," said Twilight with a shrug.

"Is it because he's a stallion? I can be a

stallion!" Discord snapped his claw and transformed into a taupe Unicorn with a black mane and a tornado cutie mark. "See?" Discord snapped his claw and switched back to his normal draconequus body.

"No, it's not that," said Fluttershy, stepping forward. "It's…it's…"

"It's what, dear Fluttershy?" Discord asked as he leaned down to the yellow Pegasus. He whipped around and began pacing back and forth across the room, counting his possible flaws on his claws. "Was I off-key? Did I not *entertain*? Were my chocolate raindrops not dazzling enough? Not chocolaty enough? Honestly, you ponies wouldn't know pure talent if it splashed you in the muzzle!" Suddenly, a gigantic bucket of water appeared out of nowhere and drenched the ponies and Spike.

"Hey! That wasn't *nice*!" Pinkie Pie shrieked, her once poufy mane now slick and dripping against her face. "You mentioned chocolate and that was WATER!"

"Discord," Twilight interrupted in a gentle tone. "I want to be honest with you, because that's what friends do." Twilight looked to Applejack for reassurance. She nodded her brown cowpony hat, and Twilight continued. "You're new to Ponyville, and that's great! But your moving here has ruffled more than a few feathers. In fact, nopony wanted to let you be in our show at all...."

"They didn't?" Discord wilted. "But I *have* to be in the show—"

"Except us," Fluttershy chimed in with a tiny grin.

"*We* stood up for you," Rarity added, trying to magic her purple mane back to its normal perfect curl. "Though now I'm starting to regret that decision. Look at my mane! It's all wet!"

"But…" Discord blasted a gust of air at the ponies, and suddenly they were dry. "Doesn't everypony like me now? I've been reformed by your 'Magic of Friendship' and all that other nonsensically hooey-gooey pony stuff that you all live by." He slumped down into a chair and slurped his cup of tea.

"While the seven of us know you've turned over a new leaf," Twilight explained, "not everypony in town knows that side of you…yet."

"I did notice a few ponies avoiding me today," Discord admitted.

"It's okay!" Spike walked over and chimed in. "The musical will be your chance to prove you don't need the spotlight!"

"That's right," Applejack said with a nod. "You can show 'em just how much you want to be a part of the Ponyville Players *and* our town by joinin' the ensemble."

"The ensemble?!" Discord spit out a gulp of tea in disgust. Fortunately, Rarity hopped out of the way just in time to avoid the stream of lukewarm water. "But if I'm in the ensemble…that means I'll have to stand *behind* the action with all the other *background ponies*, completely unnoticed by all in attendance, including Princess Celestia!" He pointed his nose skyward and crossed his arms over his brown chest. "It's hardly worth the effort at all if she doesn't watch me perform."

"Remember," Fluttershy said, trotting over to Discord, "there are no small parts, only small ponies."

"Or in this case...small draconequuses," joked Rainbow Dash. "Or is it *draconequui?*" Rainbow scratched her head. "Are there even any more of you out there?"

"Wrong!" said Discord. He pointed at Fluttershy's empty teacup, and suddenly he was sitting inside it, the size of a small garden lizard. "*Now* I'm a small draconequus." Fluttershy's eyes grew wide with surprise. Discord leaned over the rim of the cup and chuckled. "That was hilarious, because I'm physically small now." None of the ponies laughed.

"Oh, forget it," Discord pointed a claw at himself, and he was back to normal, standing next to Rainbow Dash. "I crack myself up, I really do."

"Me too!" said Pinkie Pie. "Want to hear my joke about the chicken who won the lottery?"

"Was it her *clucky day*?" Discord asked, leaning toward Pinkie Pie with his snaggle-toothed grin.

"Yeah, it was." Pinkie giggled.

"You seem to be feeling better about all this, Discord," Twilight said as she trotted to the front door. "And I'm glad. But there will be plenty of time for jokes later. We have to get things ready for our first rehearsal tomorrow. Come on, everypony!" She flung the door open and used her magic to unfurl a slide from the floating house back down to the ground. Twilight jumped out, followed by Rainbow Dash, Applejack, Pinkie Pie, Rarity, and Spike.

"Wheeeee!" Pinkie Pie squealed all the way down.

"See you tomorroooow!" shouted Spike.

"Oh no, you won't," Discord mumbled to himself. If those ponies thought he was actually going to go along with their casting decision, they were crazy. Discord had much better things to do with his time, like wreaking havoc and causing chaos. Celestia's little request wasn't worth this humiliation.

"I'm proud of you for joining our show, even though you didn't get the role you wanted," said Fluttershy with a smile. "I just had to tell you that before I go." Then she took off flying out of the door and soared toward Ponyville. As Discord watched her disappear into the distance, he got that strange feeling again. It was warm and nice. *Friendship.* It could make even a draconequus do silly things. Like join an ensemble, when he definitely deserved to be the star.

Chapter

8

Instrumental to the Show

★ ★ ★

Though Discord still felt incredibly insulted that the Ponyville Players refused to recognize his talent by awarding him the musical's lead role, he decided that he would go check out the first rehearsal anyway—just to see what a disaster it was going to be. And if it wasn't a disaster, he would be sure to spice things up. *Maybe that's why Celestia sent me here,* he thought. *To stop these ponies from being so dreadfully boring.*

"Whoa! You showed up after all," Rainbow Dash marveled, flapping her blue wings to catch up to Discord as he floated past town hall. "I was pretty sure you were going to skedaddle as soon as you got that casting news."

"Really, Rainbow Dash? Frankly, I am shocked." Discord scoffed. He twisted his long, snakelike body around and turned toward her. "You make it sound as if I have an ego as fragile as Rarity's."

"I resent that comment very much," huffed Rarity, who had been trotting behind them alongside Applejack. Rarity stuck her nose in the air, flipped her purple mane, and pushed her way forward.

"See what I mean?" Discord said. "So *touchy*." Discord and Rainbow Dash filed inside the theater and took their seats in the auditorium. The ponies who were already sitting nearby saw Discord and scurried off. It was the same old story. Nopony wanted to be near him.

"All right, Twilight. Everypony's here now," Torch Song said. She held up a scroll filled with names. Her little magenta mane braid kept swinging into her face as she spoke. "Is it time to start practicing our first scene?" She trotted over to Twilight, who was up onstage ready to give her first rehearsal pep talk.

"Thank you, Torch Song. And yes!" Twilight replied, shielding her eyes from the stage lights and looking out into the audience to greet her cast. "But...where is everypony?" Just a moment before, the entire cast and crew of *The Singing Stallion* had been awaiting instructions from their director. Now the theater was empty, except for Rainbow Dash and Discord. The big beast lounged back across several seats with his feet kicked up, nonchalantly flipping through a songbook and humming a tune. Everypony else was cowering in the shadows on either side of the room, whispering to one another in fear.

Discord sighed and closed his songbook. "The cheese stands alone, it appears."

"Cheese Sandwich?!" shouted Pinkie Pie. "Where is he? You don't have to stand alone, Cheese! I'll stand with you." She began to bounce around, searching high and low for her buddy.

"Discord." Twilight groaned. "What did you do?" Discord floated up to the stage with his claw and paw up in surrender. "Nothing at all, except *help*." He held up the songbook and pointed to a page. "This song in the show called for 'fifty-six trombones in the huge parade', so I thought I would start getting the props ready and conjure some up. That's all." He put on his most innocent face. But a subtle, wicked smile still found its way there, curling up the corners of his mouth.

Suddenly, a resounding *honk* blared through the audience. It was a giant, red trombone with a green apple on it. Twilight Sparkle narrowed her eyes. It looked familiar, somehow. "Oh my Celestia! Is that...Big Mac?!" Twilight gritted her teeth. "Did you just transform our lead actor into an instrument?!"

"Whoopsies!" Discord smiled sheepishly.

"My brother!" cried Apple Bloom, bounding over with her little bow bouncing in her mane.

"I assure you he's fine, Apple Boot." Discord giggled with glee. "But doesn't he look delightfully silly?"

"It's you who looks silly!" Apple Bloom ran over to Discord and stomped her hooves on the ground. "Change him back into a pony! RIGHT. NOW."

"Oh, fine," Discord pointed his claw at the trombone. With a zap, Big Mac was back to normal, scratching his orange mane in confusion. The rest of the ponies ran over to him to make sure he was okay. "But can I be honest with you? As your friend? You all really need to lighten up. We're *entertainers*; we're here to *entertain*."

"You promised that if we let him join our show, he wouldn't mess with us, Twilight!" shouted Minuette. She pointed her hoof at Discord. "And he's already causing trouble."

"He's going to ruin our musical!" cried Flitter.

The ponies nodded in agreement, and a buzz of activity broke out. Fluttershy and Applejack rushed onstage to help Twilight calm down the group. "All right now, everypony," said Applejack. "Let's stop overreactin'. Big Mac is jus' fine. Right?"

"Eeeeyup," Big Mac said with a cool nod.

"Discord's just nervous, is all," Fluttershy replied, her voice soft. "He's still new to

Ponyville, and you're all being very hard on him. Please give him another chance." She shot a serious look at Discord. He cowered. "I think you should apologize now, Discord. That was a very mean thing to do."

"I'm so very sorry, Large Macintosh," Discord said, bowing deep and draping his lion's arm across his body. "Please accept this trombone as recompense for my thoughtless actions." Discord passed Big Mac a shiny yellow trombone.

Apple Bloom's jaw dropped. "Who is that?!"

"Nopony, that one's actually just a trombone. But you should have seen your face. Priceless!" Discord held his stomach and laughed hysterically.

"That's quite enough playing around," Twilight chided. "We've got an actual play to do, remember? Rehearsal was supposed to start three minutes ago."

Discord yawned, pointed to his watch, and looked around. "Well, what's been taking so long? Let's put on a musical!"

Chapter

9

Bursting Discord's Bubble

★ ★ ★

Once things got rolling with the show, Discord felt himself nicely settling into his new life in Ponyville. He would visit Fluttershy's house for tea, shop for groceries at the Ponyville market, and once he even went to Twilight Sparkle's castle to borrow a book on Bridleway musicals. He often saw

Martingale shuffling about town, having heated conversations with other ponies or giving Discord the side-eye.

When there was only a week left until Princess Celestia would be visiting to watch the Ponyville Players production of *The Singing Stallion*, Discord was feeling confident in his secret plan to steal the show. Predictably, Princess Twilight Sparkle was a bundle of nerves, eager to show her superiors how well the community in Ponyville was flourishing under the flag of friendship. She didn't suspect a thing.

Luckily, everypony else was too busy to notice as well. On top of learning their parts in the show, many of the ponies also helped with the logistics. Applejack had delivered some beautiful wooden sets, not unlike the ones she had once built for a

Manehattan community play. Rarity had measured, sewn, and trimmed everypony's costumes to perfection. Rainbow Dash did her part by enlisting Flitter and Cloudchaser to help her create some trick weather effects that would enhance the show but wouldn't ruin the theater. Pinkie Pie kept busy designing posters and balloons that advertised the show all over town and beyond. And Fluttershy took charge of the accompaniment—recruiting all the best musicians to become their very own Ponyville Players orchestra for the run of the production.

One afternoon, the lights were up and the whole cast was onstage. It had taken many long rehearsals to place everypony in their spots, blocking all the scenes one by one, so it was very important that the cast members not make any mistakes. Twilight sat in the audience next to Applejack and Spike, calling out all the cues, marks, and cutie marks.

"Everypony ready?" she projected out to the stage. "Let's take it from the ensemble chorus of the song 'Bubbles' in Act One. The part right after Professor Hayloft Shill has shown the town of Glimmer City how much fun the bubbles can be. Then we'll go straight into my favorite scene—the library romance with Mare-ion Pear."

Davenport stomped a beat with his back left hoof and began the song, hitting the large keys of his pony piano. *Plink-plonk, plinkity-plonk. Plink, plonk.*

"*Bubbles! Oh, we got bubbles, right here in Glimmer City!*" the ensemble sang. "*With a capital* B *that rhymes with* C *and that stands for* COOL!" Discord swayed back and forth to the music with the rest of the cast. He didn't really blend in. It was nearly impossible to do so, since he was three times taller than the tallest pony in the ensemble, Senior Mint. But as Discord sang with the ponies, he stepped in time, tapped, and twirled. Pinkie Pie stood in the wings and blew rainbow-colored bubbles into the air onto the dancers. Downstage, Big Mac paced across the stage and began singing.

"Yes, that stands for cool!" sang Big Mac in his deep baritone voice. *"We've got—"*

Discord had been practicing the role of Hayloft Shill in secret, and suddenly he found himself unable to resist the urge to perform. He twirled into the center of the scene, singing the next verse with Big Mac. *"We've got all these bubbles! All around in Glimmer City, all around! Gotta come up with a way, to keep those bubbles at play—because they rule! Bubbles, bubbles, bubbles, bubbles!"*

The music came to a halt, and everypony looked at Discord, annoyed.

"What are you doing, Discord?" Cheerilee asked in her gentlest tone, usually reserved for teaching the colts and fillies at school. She looked concerned. "Are you okay?"

"I simply felt the song could be improved upon," Discord replied, throwing his paw and claw into the air in surrender. *"Oopsies."*

"You're always holding us up," muttered a big, blue stallion named Noteworthy. "We can't even run through a whole number without you adding your own flair one way or another." Noteworthy trotted over to Discord and puffed out his chest. "If you ask me, I think you're trying to sabotage this show!"

A flurry of whispers broke out at the accusation. Discord rolled his yellow eyes. "Don't insult me, pony. If I wanted to do that, I could do a lot more than sing a few extra parts. I'm the king of chaos, remember?" Discord began to cackle at the absurdity of the situation. Everypony took a few steps back, suddenly fearful.

Noteworthy narrowed his eyes. "Then what *are* you doing here? Why would somepony as powerful as you want to be in a small-town musical?"

"Isn't it obvious?" Discord whipped out a display filled with a giant line graph. He procured a wooden pointing stick and tapped it on the bottom. "Ever since I learned about friendship from Fluttershy and her pals, my approval rating has been rising at a healthy rate. If I portray myself in a positive light with the ponies of Ponyville through the power of song and dance, then it will only continue to grow!"

"Oh," said Pinkie Pie, tilting her head to the side. "I just thought you really liked show tunes."

"That, too," giggled Discord. He turned to the stage full of his castmates. "Anyway, I didn't mean to get so carried away. I won't do it again, I promise." Discord shrunk himself down to Spike's size for effect. "I'll stay back here in my little spot." Everypony trotted back to their original places to run through the number again.

Applejack gave Davenport a nod, and the piano began.

"Oh, we got bubbles!" sang the chorus, just as before. *"Right here in Glimmer City!"* Big Mac shuffled out to the front to sing his line, but Discord stayed put. He danced in the back, minding his own business and doing his choreography. That's why it came as such a surprise when, instead of singing, Big Mac started burping up bubbles! His eyes went wide with shock, and everypony whipped around to face Discord.

"Oh, Discord," Rarity said, putting a hoof to her face in exasperation. "Whatever have you done *now*?"

Discord's jaw dropped. "Nothing! I-I..." he stammered. He was speechless. Because for the first time, a prank actually had been played by somepony else. And now the joke was on *him*!

Chapter

10

Funny Business

★ ★ ★

When he arrived back at his chaotic little cottage, all Discord wanted was to be alone. But another pony was already there waiting for him, pacing back and forth on the ground below the floating abode. "What do you want?" Discord snapped, floating up to the porch. He was in a foul mood after being thrown out of rehearsal by the other ponies. They really thought he'd given Big Mac the bubble-hiccups.

"To talk to you about vacatin' the premises," Martingale grumbled. "*Again*. You have to leave! Everypony in town is mad at me for lettin' you move into this house. They say it's been nothin' but chaos since you arrived in Ponyville."

"For the first time in my life, I can say that is complete hogwash." Discord sighed. "Now please go away. I have to go sulk."

"Your little play not going so well?" Martingale asked with a satisfied smirk. "Heard there was some funny business goin' on today, and it was all caused by you."

"That is *not* true!" Discord shot back. "I only caused *some* of the funny business. Somepony else finished it off, and now the whole cast thinks I can't be trusted. It's dreadful." Discord sat down on his front steps and put his lion's paw under his chin in defeat. "Oh, Mr. Nightingale, I've just been trying to fit in here, and everypony still thinks I'm a monster." Discord pictured his prize, buried deep in a guarded basement room at Canterlot Castle. "What would Celestia say? Surely she won't reward me for a job poorly done.…"

Martingale perked up. "So you thinkin' you might leave Ponyville now?"

"No, of course not," Discord scoffed.

"But you must! Don't you see?" Martingale stomped his hooves in frustration. "My business is ruined! Nopony will work with me until I get you to leave."

"As sad as your little tale of woe is, I simply cannot concede." Discord shrugged.

"I made a commitment to be in *The Singing Stallion*. And so, the show must go on." He posed with his lion's paw over his heart and looked off into the horizon.

"I was 'fraid you'd say that." Martingale shook his head. He turned on his hoof and trotted off with a sad look on his face. "Guess I'm gonna have to take matters into my own hooves again," he muttered under his breath.

A few moments later, a group of ponies crossed paths with the disgruntled stallion. It was strange how he didn't even wave or say hello. "Sheesh! What's wrong with him?" asked Rainbow Dash, looking back over her shoulder.

"Somepony's got the grump-grumps!" Pinkie Pie added. "Maybe he hasn't had a cupcake today." She turned around, bounced over to him, and was back within ten seconds. "Worse than I thought! Red velvet, you guys. He refused *red velvet*."

"Well, it looks like he just came from Discord's house," Twilight pointed out, looking uneasy. "Maybe he's been up to something worse in Ponyville than making ponies burp bubbles."

Chapter

11

The Pony of Shadows

★ ★ ★

As she waited for the actors to arrive, Twilight Sparkle stood onstage, basking in the sight of the beautiful library. Even though it was all a set—wooden planks propped up and painted to look like towering shelves of dusty books—it still made her feel safe and comfortable. She smiled, fondly remembering her old home: the Golden Oak Library. The cozy book-filled tree had been destroyed in an epic battle against Tirek, aided by Discord's powerful magic. She missed it very much.

Twilight thought it was such a shame that the draconequus had been swayed by Tirek to turn against friendship, falling back into his old ways even for a brief time. She wondered if perhaps he was sliding back into bad habits once more. Either way, the princess had her eye on Discord. Nothing was going to stand in the way of Ponyville's big theater debut.

After the bubble incident, it seemed everypony else was waiting for the other horseshoe to drop, too. Noteworthy had taken to following him around, hoping for some morsel of dirt to tell the others. But

Discord was a model cast member! He showed up to rehearsals on time and did his best not to steal the spotlight, even when he was doing an amazing dance or belting out a song. When it wasn't his line, Discord only spoke up if a pony had forgotten their part. It was actually quite helpful.

Nopony had ever seen Fluttershy so smug before. She loved to see all of Discord's neighsayers proven wrong. "When you show somepony kindness," she would remind them, "they will know kindness and offer it in return! Even Discord. He's just a big softie, really." That part always made Angel roll his little eyes. The bunny hadn't gotten over Discord's pranks, either.

Twilight was broken from her reverie by the sounds of voices and hooves outside the theater entrance. The doors flung open, and a flurry of activity began. "Twilight, dear!" Rarity called out, trotting in with two racks of costumes. "The Trotting Band uniforms for the final scene have been altered and cleaned in time for dress rehearsals. Don't they look utterly *fabulous*?"

"Stunning as always, Rarity," Twilight said with a sincere nod. "Line them up backstage in the dressing rooms."

"And I've got the hats!" added Spike, scurrying in behind her. He swayed back and forth under the weight of a stack of hats twice as tall as him. The little dragon leaned around the hats, which were blocking his vision. "Rarity, wait up!" A few hats from the top tumbled down as he rushed to follow her.

"Welcome, everypony," said Twilight Sparkle as the rest of the cast members trickled into the theater one by one. "Please, take a seat!" They gossiped and giggled with nervous energy. There was a buzz in the air. It was an electric feeling that only seemed to happen when there was less than a week until "curtains up." Soon, all of their hard work would be on display for everypony in town to see.

"Let's all pipe down now, so Twilight can say her part and we can get things movin'!" Applejack shouted to the ponies.

"Thanks, A.J.," Twilight said. "Okay, Ponyville Players…" She began pacing the stage as she spoke. "It's dress rehearsal week. That means we need to be *even more* focused than before! Remember your costume changes and all your cues, and we should be in great shape to put on an amazing show."

"Please don't forget your accessories!" Rarity added. "They really do complete each look."

"Anypony have questions?" Rainbow Dash called out. Discord raised his claw, but she ignored him. "No? Okay, great. Let's *do* this."

The draconequus cleared his throat. "*Ahem!* Over here!"

"Yes, Discord?" Fluttershy asked, ever patient.

"It's not really a question, it's more of a *suggestion....*" Discord explained, standing up. He looked around at the faces of the other ponies. "Am I the only one who thinks the choreography at the end of Act One is severely *lacking?*"

"Lackin' in what?" questioned Apple Bloom, raising a brow and cocking her head to the side.

"Oomph!" Discord replied. "Zing!"

"Pizzazz?" finished Pinkie Pie with a grin.

"Precisely."

Noteworthy stood up. "We don't have time to practice a new routine. I think it's just fine the way it is." He turned to Big Mac, Senior Mint, Toe Tapper, Spike, and Davenport for support. "Don't you, fellas?"

"Eeyup," Big Mac agreed.

"Definitely," said Senior Mint.

"Uhh…" Spike hesitated. "I think…" He looked to Discord, who has his arms across his chest. He was tapping his green hoof on the floor impatiently. Spike turned to Twilight Sparkle for guidance. He didn't want to get on the bad side of the king of chaos. "Maybe it *could* use something else?"

Suddenly, the theater lights began to flicker. The whole room turned pitch black. In the dark, a wave of whispers echoed through the cast, accompanied by the shuffling and stomping of hooves. "Hey!" shouted somepony. "What happened?"

Spike waved his claws in front of him to make sure nopony was there. He blew some fire into the air. For a brief moment, he thought he saw a pony slipping through the back door. But it could have just been a shadow.

"Oh, calm down." Discord snapped his claw, and the hooflights came on. Everything was illuminated once more. *POP!* A light burnt out, smoke rising from the shattered bulb. *POP! POP! POP!* Three more followed. A creepy tune began to play on the piano, even though Davenport was nowhere near it. It grew louder and louder as the ponies stepped back. Soon they were huddled in the center of the room in a big group.

Flitter and Noteworthy exchanged a nervous look. Everypony turned to face Discord. "Very strange, indeed," said the draconequus, rubbing his white beard. He clapped his paw and claw together three times, and the music stopped. "I know what you're all thinking." He sighed. "But I didn't do it."

"Then who *did*?" Apple Bloom trotted over to inspect the burned-out lights.

"Beats me!" Discord pointed at the broken lights and sent a zap of blue magic over to them. They were immediately fixed. "Perhaps it was a pony ghostie?" Discord quipped with a chuckle.

Torch Song's eyes widened. "The Pony of Shadows?!" Everypony started talking at once. Granny Smith had passed around the mysterious legend of the dark, magical creature all over Ponyville. But Twilight, who knew better, was growing impatient.

"Enough! That's just an old mare's tale." She trotted back over to center stage and turned to the group. "And the lights are fixed now, so it's time for us to work. Now let's take a look at that final song in Act One before we do a full run-through." Twilight winked at Discord. His face broke into a little smile.

As the ponies obliged, filing onto the stage and taking their places, they shot suspicious glances over at Discord. He was used to this sort of treatment, but it hurt a teensy bit to think that none of the cast members trusted him. After all, he'd been *so good* lately.

Noteworthy was the last to trot up the stairs. As he did, he leaned in near Discord's ear and whispered, "I've got my eye on you...." It made Discord want to cause some trouble, just to put that sneaky pony back in his place! He felt himself growing weak, his hands just itching for mischief.

Discord couldn't resist when he had the brilliant idea to turn the stage into an ice rink halfway through the song and dance. Instead of doing their choreography, the ponies began to slip and slide across the stage at random. "Wheeee!" squealed Pinkie Pie, twirling around in glee. Discord giggled at the chaos of it all.

Unfortunately, nopony else thought it was very funny. Fluttershy looked disappointed, and Twilight was forced to dismiss him from the rest of rehearsal. As Discord left the theater, he could hear his favorite song from the show playing. He slumped down, torn between his true nature and his obligation to the ponies and Princess Celestia. Maybe he shouldn't have pulled that ice stunt. But it was almost worth it just to see Noteworthy fall flat on his flank.

Chapter

12

The Disguise

★ ★ ★

The ponies and Spike had only been inside Discord's house for a few moments when he broke down into a puddle of emotion. "Okay, okay—I confess!" Discord blubbered, head down on the kitchen table. "It's true! I have been keeping a secret from you all. I was only doing the play because Princess Celestia sent me on a mission to test my friendship skills, and said I had to!" He gasped and covered his mouth.

"Uh...we didn't even ask ya anything yet." Applejack looked to her friends, eyebrow cocked. They seemed as equally puzzled as she was. "But I applaud yer honesty?"

"Princess Celestia gives *you* tests, too?" Twilight was dumbfounded. "How long has this been going on? Who else is involved?" She began to pace back and forth on the uneven floor, racking her brain for answers. Even though Twilight Sparkle was no longer the princess's faithful student, she still couldn't give up the idea of being the only teacher's pet. "I must write to her and catch up...."

"Twilight, aren't you forgetting why we came over here in the first place?" Rainbow Dash urged. She bit her lip. "You know…"

"Oh, right." Twilight straightened and cleared her throat. "Discord—in light of your recent confession, this makes things rather awkward but…"

"The cast of *The Singing Stallion* think it might be best if you sit this one out," Apple-jack admitted. "Real sorry, sugarcube."

"I'm *out* of the show?!" Discord wailed. "Why?"

"They all think you're just playing a big prank on them," Spike shrugged. He held out his left claw and counted on it. "First, there was the trombone thing, then it was the bubble burps, then the hooflights and the creepy music, then the ice rink stage, and *then* the ruined library set!"

"But I didn't do all those things!" Discord retorted. "Only two of them."

"See?" said Fluttershy, turning to the others with a proud smile. "I knew he would never ruin your set, Applejack."

"But if you didn't, then who did?" Rarity asked.

"I haven't the foggiest idea." Suddenly, a small cloud of fog rolled in through the open window and surrounded the top of Discord's head like a hat. He closed his eyes and thought for a moment. "It must have been that pony, Noteworthy!" Discord nodded, rubbing his white goatee with his claw. "That fellow sure does dislike me."

Pinkie Pie shook her head. "What a bunch of dramarama!"

Discord wasn't sure what to do. He had

really made quite the mess with all his antics at rehearsal. "Normally, a petty little pony activity wouldn't concern me in the slightest," he whined. "But I've actually become quite attached to the idea of being onstage. It made me feel included."

"And we loved having you there, too," assured Fluttershy. She looked down at the ground, defeated. Her pink mane fell in front of her eyes. "I just wish there was some way for you to be in the show without upsetting everypony."

"Like wear a disguise?" asked Pinkie Pie.

"That's brilliant!" Discord popped up to his feet. "I can be in the show *and* investigate who framed me so I can clear my name." The draconequus disappeared into a puff of smoke. When it cleared, there stood a taupe Unicorn with a black mane and a tornado cutie mark. Discord the pony grinned. "It's showtime!"

Chapter

13

Discord's Secret Debut

★ ★ ★

Twilight Sparkle stood center stage. The entire Ponyville Players cast was gathered one last time before the big show that evening. She looked out to their excited, nervous faces and smiled.

"Well, ponies—this is it!" The ponies all hooted, hollered, and stomped their hooves on the ground to applaud. "Before I let you all go and get ready backstage, I have an important announcement." Twilight motioned for the pony-disguised Discord to stand by her side. He trotted over. "This is Tony Stanza. He just happened to be passing through town on his way back from Manehattan, where he was performing in a Bridleway revival of *Les Miser Stables* with Countess Coloratura! He has kindly offered to take Discord's place in the ensemble. Though, I still hope you'll consider inviting Discord back to the cast...." Discord was thrilled. Twilight never second-guessed Tony's story at all.

"No way! Right, everypony?" shouted Noteworthy. "He would have embarrassed us in front of the other princesses with one of his tricks!" The ponies all nodded and murmured in agreement, still clearly convinced that they knew who was to blame. Twilight looked to Discord, worried his feelings might be hurt. But instead, he looked oddly thrilled.

"I'm proud of each and every one of you," announced the princess. "Enjoy yourselves tonight, and break a hoof!"

It was a fully packed house. The audience was buzzing with enthusiasm as friends from near and far greeted one another and found their seats. The soft sounds of the Ponyville Orchestra warming up their instruments added to the ambience. Rarity stood backstage and pressed her white cheek up to the curtains to peek through, taking extra care not to smudge her heavy stage makeup on the red velvet fabric. "Oh, my stars! Everypony who's anypony is here tonight. There's Princess Celestia and Princess Luna...and the Wonderbolts...and Coco Pommel!"

"Wow! I guess my balloon-o-gram invitations really worked, huh?" Pinkie Pie said, looking satisfied. "Is my sister out there?"

Rarity scanned the crowd. "Hmmm, well, there's Hoity Toity...and there's Tree Hugger....Oh! There she is!"

Pinkie Pie popped her head out next to Rarity's and immediately saw her older sister, Maud Pie, sitting near the back. The gray pony with a light purple mane had an expression on her face completely devoid of emotion. "Awww, she's so excited to see me perform," Pinkie cooed.

Over on the other side of the wings, Pony Discord peeked out from the curtain as well. He stared at Princess Celestia, wondering if she would know that it was him in the show and that he'd kept up with his secret friendship mission. Either way, he decided, it would be fine. He was just glad to be performing tonight with his new Ponyville pals.

"Hey there!" Noteworthy trotted up to join him. He was wearing his costume—a jaunty waistcoat and straw hat. "Tony Stanza, right?"

"Indeed," replied Discord, narrowing his eyes at the pony responsible for turning the others against him. "So, if I may ask...what happened to the poor chap who needed a last-minute understudy?"

"He was a great singer and dancer, but he kept trying to ruin the scenes with all these silly jokes and pranks," Noteworthy explained. "He wasn't being a team player."

Twilight Sparkle trotted past with her clipboard. "Five minutes, everypony! Five minutes to curtain!"

"Are you sure he was responsible for all the pranks?" Pony Discord pried, taking a few steps closer to the blue stallion. "What if it was somepony else who tried to *frame* him?"

"Couldn't be. He causes chaos wherever he goes. Who else could have played those pranks?" Noteworthy made a funny face and looked at Pony Discord a little closer. "Why are you so interested in this anyway?"

"No reason," replied Pony Discord. He was sure that this was his stallion. The guy had guilt written all over him. The wheels in Discord's head were already turning, trying to come up with a way to get back at him. "I suppose we should take our places for the first scene."

"Break a hoof!" Noteworthy said, tipping his hat and trotting onstage.

"Yes, you too...." said Pony Discord, a devious smile forming on his face. All he had to do was wait for the right moment to embarrass him.

Chapter

14

Showstoppers

★ ★ ★

The first act flew by without a hitch. As the curtain lowered down for intermission, Discord couldn't believe it. He'd been having so much fun that he'd completely forgotten about all the drama. Everypony was busy congratulating one another on a great job so far when Discord noticed a strange-looking pony with aa mustache dressed all in black. The stallion was climbing a ladder up to the rafters and kept looking back over his shoulder.

Pony Discord nudged Big Mac. "Do you recognize that stagehoof?"

"Nope," he said before heading off to change his costume.

"Everypony needs to hurry and get into their clothes for Act Two!" Twilight hollered. "That means you, too, Dis—I mean Tony Stanza!"

By the time Discord returned to the stage wearing his new costume, the mysterious pony was gone. Senior Mint, who was in charge of the props, trotted up and passed Pony Discord a trombone and a Trotting Band hat with a red feather plume.

"Did you happen to notice a mustachioed stagehoof hanging around here?" Discord asked. "I think he was up to something...."

"Only stagehoof we have is Bulk Biceps," said Senior Mint, pointing his hoof at the muscular white Pegasus with tiny wings.

Sure enough, he was dressed in all black and was busy lifting a gigantic wooden set piece all by himself. "Yeaaaaaaaaaah!" he grunted, hoisting it onto one shoulder.

"How peculiar," mumbled Discord. "Who is that other pony?"

"Places, everypony!" shouted Rainbow Dash, flying to her own spot for the big Trotting Band scene. "This is gonna be awesome!" The cast scurried across the stage, finding their marks. Discord followed, still trying to figure out if the stallion he'd seen was a figment of his overactive imagination.

The curtain rose, and bright lights illuminated the stage.

"Fifty-six trombones in the pony parade, with two hundred and ten plump hens close at hoof!" sang the ensemble, trotting in time across the stage. A bunch of chicken-shaped balloons bobbed alongside them. *"They were followed by rows of crows flying up above the show, it was a dream for all across the laaand!"* Discord blew into his trombone and began to play. The music rose, and it was time for Cheerilee and Big Mac's final duet.

As he marched to the back of the stage for the last formation, Discord happened to glance up at the rafters. The stagehoof was there! The gent was using his Unicorn magic to gently lift a bucket of something, tilting it toward the stage. As soon as he saw the substance catch the light, he realized what it was. Discord dived toward Cheerilee and Big Mac, shoving them out of the spotlight. "Nooo!"

He made it just in time to get an entire bucket of sparkly sneeze dust poured onto him instead. "Achoooo!" Pony Discord sneezed. The audience gasped. Discord looked down at his hooves—which now appeared to be a claw and a paw. He had become his normal self again! He froze on the spot, looking out at the shocked faces of the audience, not knowing what to do. Then he sneezed again, and he was back to his Pony Discord form. Suddenly, everypony onstage was sneezing in time to the music.

It was so silly that the audience laughed and started to cheer, stomping in time to the music.

Discord laughed, too. He conjured up some of his draconequus magic to lift the sneeze dust off the actors and made it swirl up above them into beautiful patterns in time to the music. Everypony began their dance again, and Discord took the opportunity to magically lower the culprit from the rafters.

Nopony was more shocked than Discord to see it was Martingale—the real estate pony! Martingale looked around in a panic for an exit, but they were all blocked. Discord smirked and made the pony join in the dance by using his magic to force Martingale to move like a marionette.

To the audience, it all appeared as part of the show.

When it finally ended, the applause was thunderous. Discord had accidentally stolen a piece of the show.

Chapter

15

A Friend to Ponykind

★ ★ ★

Discord's house was bursting at the seams with ponies. The whole cast and half the audience had shown up at the impromptu after-show soiree to celebrate. Princess Celestia and Princess Luna were even in attendance, sipping dainty teacups full of apple cider and conversing with Twilight Sparkle and her friends.

As Discord bounced around the rooms, he felt full of pride and happiness. He'd done what Celestia had wished by joining the Ponyville community, and in the process, he'd made some new friends. Discord pushed past Lyra and Berry Punch to the kitchen, retrieved three mugs of cider, and brought them outside to the front garden. Thankfully, the house was now on the actual ground again.

"Martingale! Noteworthy!" Discord called out. "A toast!" He used his magic to pass the mugs over. "Can you believe what we put everypony through just because of our little disagreement? This whole time, *Martingale* was the one scheming to frame me and get me kicked out of town. I really thought it was you, Noteworthy." Discord laughed. "I love it when ponies surprise me! Well done."

"I guess we both kind of were," Noteworthy admitted. "Sorry…"

"Me too," added Martingale with a shrug. "I was just so angry when everypony in town started blamin' me for stuff you'd done around town. I figured the only way to get ya to move back out was to ruin your part in the play."

"No, it is *I* who should be apologizing," Discord said with a bow. "I should have never squatted in this house, and I should have been kinder to the Ponyville Players. I was just so worried that if I wasn't the center of attention, I wouldn't be noticed at all.

But then I came to realize how pleasant it is *not* to have everything revolve around you! Who knew?" Discord took a pensive sip of his cider. "Everything is a team effort here in Ponyville. Just fascinating…"

"I was hoping you would feel that way, Discord," said Princess Celestia, walking over to join them. Princess Luna followed. Discord and the two stallions bowed to the royals. Celestia smiled. "And I have to say, you surprised me, too. Excellent performance in *The Singing Stallion*, and as a pony as well!" The sisters shared a chuckle.

"Being a pony is not so terrible," Discord said, rolling his eyes. "But I'm still glad I'm not one."

"As long as you are a true friend to ponykind, that is enough. It will always be enough." Celestia bent down and conjured up a swirl of glittering pink magic from her horn. "I believe I owe you something." Suddenly, an object appeared that looked like a ball carved from stone.

"Finally!" Discord exclaimed. "I've looked everywhere for this."

Celestia wore a baffled expression. "I'm unaware of what this object is, but I know that it means a great deal to you. You only put your Crest of Chaos on your most valued possessions, if I recall."

"Too right, Princess," Discord agreed, holding the stone ball close to his chest. He whispered something, and a swirl of multicolored magic enveloped the dracon-equus and his treasure. When the color dissipated, the object had transformed into a fishbowl! There was a little white and orange fish splashing around inside.

"Quincy!" Discord cried out, gathering it in a tight embrace. "It's been so long! I've missed you."

Fluttershy noticed right away. She came over and peered into the bowl. "Awww, who's this little sweetie?"

"My clownfish, Quincy," Discord explained like a proud parent. "But I like to call him Q. It feels so good to be reunited. I do believe there's just one thing missing...."

"What's that?" asked Twilight Sparkle, turning her attention away from Rainbow Dash, Pinkie Pie, Rarity, Spike, and Applejack.

"Home!" Discord laughed and looked down at the happy fish. "Come on, Q. Martingale found a buyer for our Ponyville house. Let's go back to where it's normal."

Then he gave a wink, turned on his heel, and headed in the direction of Chaosville.

As soon as he was out of sight, Discord's face suddenly materialized in the reflection of everypony's drinks, giving them all a fright. "Boo! See you for next year's show, Ponyville Players! This time I better get the lead...or else!" he shouted and then broke into his famous cackle. "Just kidding! But you should have seen your faces!"

Read them all!

Turn the page for
a special surprise
from Discord!

Dear reader,

I put together these bonus pages just for you! Have fun filling them out and Sharing them with your friends!

yours in chaos,
Discord

Juggling Ponies

Discord has so many new pony friends to keep track of!
Since he's new to friendship, he wants to give each of
his friends a gift they might enjoy, but he needs help
remembering what they like. Can you draw a line to
match each friend to his or her favorite item?

PICK YOUR PONYBILLS

Below is a list of all the shows Discord has seen on Bridleway in Manehattan. Pick your favorite one and design the Ponybill (a fancy word for program)!

HINNY OF THE HILLS   TWILIGHT EXPRESS

MANESPRAY   THE SINGING STALLION   FILLY ELLIOT

PONYBILL

MODE ABODE

All the homes in Ponyville have style, but Discord takes pride in making his the most unique one around. How would you decorate your house in Ponyville? Would you draw stripes or spots? Paint your front door purple or green? Decorate the house below to make it your own!

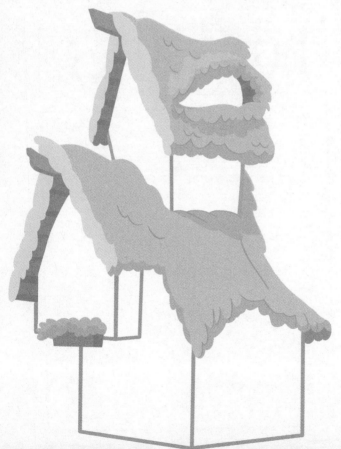

THE BLAME GAME

Discord has a reputation for creating chaos wherever he goes. When crazy things start to happen, everypony assumes he caused them, even though he's innocent! Have you ever been blamed for something you didn't do? What happened? How did you handle the situation? Write about it here.

LET'S PLAY!

The Ponyville Players love to put together performances. Have you ever been in a show? Use the space below to plan what your perfect play with your pals would be like!

TITLE

TYPE (CIRCLE ONE)

Musical   Play   Variety Show

CAST MEMBERS

Name	Part
_____	_____
_____	_____
_____	_____
_____	_____
_____	_____
_____	_____

WHAT HAPPENS IN ACT I

WHAT HAPPENS IN ACT II

ENSEMBLE ENSEMBLES

Now that you've outlined your production, it's time to design the costumes! Use the pony forms to create your characters' wardrobes!

CHAOS JUMBLE

What happens when you mix ponies with Discord? Chaos, of course! He put a curse on the letters, causing them to dance around the page. Can you help the Ponyville Players rearrange the names of these ponies for the show program?

GBI CMA

_____

LTUFREHYST

_____

YRTRAI

_____

TROHC ONSG

_____

GIVE MY REGARDS TO BRIDLEWAY

Can you find these words in the puzzle below?

audition	cast	production
backstage	curtain	rehearsal
Bridleway	musical	spotlight

```
N S N I A T R U C B R Z
E O P R E H E A R S A L
G V I O A U D I T I O N
A M X T T J D X N J Y D
T T U N C L W M Q D R N
S L M S E U I X Y N K Y
K P G W I C D G T W J T
C K A K A C Q O H J Q M
A Y D S R T A D R T B Y
B R T T L J P L T P G P
```

PONY PRIDE

Discord's best pony friend is Fluttershy. Imagine how proud she must have been to see the draconequus participate in The Singing Stallion *and learn more about the Magic of Friendship! Have you ever been proud of a friend for overcoming a challenge? Write about it here!*

_____

_____

_____

_____

_____

_____

_____

_____

AN A-MAZE-iNG PERFORMANCE

In order to get to Ponyville, Discord must first travel through the disarray of Chaosville. Can you help him find his way through the maze?

START

FINISH

SHOW TUNE SPECTACULAR

The Singing Stallion *is chock-full of toe-tapping tunes. Write the lyrics for your own hit musical here!*

_____

_____

_____

_____

_____

_____

_____

_____

_____

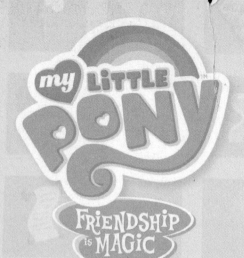

CUTIE MARK QUESTS

NOW ON DVD!

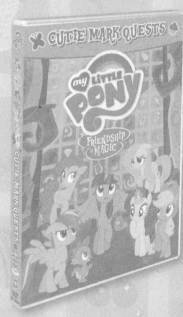